The Sleepover Club

Have you been invited to all these sleepovers?

Sleepover Girls on Safari

by Angie Bates

HarperCollins *Children's Books*

The Sleepover Club ® is a
Registered trademark of HarperCollins*Publishers* Ltd

First published in Great Britain by Collins in 2003
Collins is an imprint of HarperCollins*Publishers* Ltd
77-85 Fulham Palace Road, Hammersmith,
London W6 8JB

The HarperCollins *Children's Books* website address is
www.harpercollinschildrensbooks.co.uk

3

Text copyright © Angie Bates 2003

Original series characters, plotlines
and settings © Rose Impey 1997

ISBN 0 00 711766 3

The author asserts the moral right to
be identified as the author of the work.

Printed and bound in England by
Clays Ltd, St Ives plc

Sleepover Kit List

1. Sleeping bag
2. Pillow
3. Pyjamas or a nightdress
4. Slippers
5. Toothbrush, toothpaste, soap etc
6. Towel
7. Teddy
8. A creepy story
9. Food for a midnight feast:
   chocolate, crisps, sweets, biscuits.
   In fact anything you like to eat.
10. Torch
11. Hairbrush
12. Hair things like a bobble or hairband,
    if you need them
13. Clean knickers and socks
14. Change of clothes for the next day
15. Sleepover diary and membership card

CHAPTER ONE

Oh, hiya! Didn't see you there. I wasn't really singing into my hairbrush in front of the mirror, honest. Oh, all right, I was! But I do have a good excuse. I'm practising for this cheesy school talent contest Frankie's roped us into. I wouldn't have agreed but she said the others REALLY needed me to be their stylist. "You're the Sleepover Club fashion guru, Fliss," she cooed.

As you know, Frankie Thomas is a world expert at getting her own way and I fell for it, like I always do. Then Frankie immediately started piling on the pressure, saying it just wouldn't feel right unless ALL the Sleepover Club girls performed with her.

Then she turned her puppy dog eyes on me. "I can understand that you're nervous, Flissie," she'd said in a teacherish kind of voice. "But I don't think you'd forgive yourself if you missed out on this unique experience."

I really hate myself for giving in to her. Plus I'm stuck with having to learn this impossible S Club 7 dance routine, PLUS I've got to master the words to *Reach for the Stars*! It's a complete nightmare. I'm SO not co-ordinated. I must have tripped over my own feet five times.

Oops, listen to me wittering! Now you're terrified I'm going to make you watch us do our horrible impression of S Club 7. But don't panic! That is NOT why I asked you over, cross my heart and spit.

But I'd better warn you. By the time I've finished recounting our latest sleepover, you're probably going to have to sleep with the light on. We've got a genuinely spine-chilling experience in store for you this time.

So let's make sure the front and back doors are securely locked and bolted! Then prepare to be shocked and scandalised. Because every word I'm going to tell you is totally TOTALLY true.

It was a sunny day in spring. Outside the school dinner hall, birds zoomed to and fro and the school flowerbeds had cute little primulas and whatever poking up out of the dirt. Lyndz had just shared out those little sugarcoated mini-eggs that look like tiny, speckled bird's eggs. "I thought it would put everyone in a holiday mood," she grinned.

We'd managed to get a whole dinner table to ourselves. Alana Banana and Regina Hill hovered hopefully for a few seconds but Kenny gave them one of her stares and they quickly took the hint.

In four days' time we were going on the ultimate class trip – to have what Mrs Weaver described as a "safari experience". We'd all heard of Gawdy Castle Safari Park, but none of us had actually been, and we were getting totally overexcited.

"I can't wait," said Kenny. "Lions in the wild. Raaargh!!" She hooked her fingers into claws and waved them menacingly in Lyndz's face.

"This is going to be so amazing," I said. "Isn't it, Rosie?"

"From what I heard yesterday, Gawdy Castle might be a bit TOO amazing!" Frankie had that annoying little smirk on her face that means she's got secret inside info. "I've been talking to this kid whose sister went years ago. Boy, you should have heard what she told me."

I was suddenly completely distracted. "Not again! I've broken another nail!" I screeched. I couldn't believe my bad luck. I'd been trying to grow all my nails to the same length for weeks. Now the most exciting adventure of our lives was looming and I'd gone and ruined my Pink Passion nail-polished fingernail.

"Don't be such a bimbo, Fliss!"

I DO wish Frankie would learn not to talk with her mouth full. Gloopy egg sandwich suddenly went splattering everywhere, and poor ol' Kenny was right in the line of fire.

"Urgh, Frankie! That was so gross!" She frantically brushed yellow and white gunk off her t-shirt.

I helped Kenz mop herself up. Ever since the twins were born, I make sure I carry travel wipes in my bag, so I'm prepared for spills and dribbles of all kinds. Joe and Hannah could totally dribble for England!

Frankie joined in the mopping operation. "Sorry, Kenz," she said, "but Fliss has been banging on about her silly nails all term. We're going to Gawdy Castle in four days and there's something you guys really ought to know."

Mum reckons the other girls will catch up and learn to love lip-gloss and nail polish as much as I do. I hope she's right. Sometimes I think my mates see me as a total fluff brain. As for Frankie, she's always saying I shouldn't worry about shallow girly stuff like getting my appliquéd butterfly jeans dirty. She says it ruins everyone's fun.

I hate to think I might be the Sleepover Club party pooper, so right there in the dinner hall, I made a secret pact with myself that I would NOT be ruining our thrilling, end of term trip.

"Sorry, Frankie," I said humbly. "Tell us your story."

Frankie plans to be an actress when she grows up and she just LURVES to be the centre of attention. She took a long, very noisy sip of Snapple, to make sure everyone was watching. Then she made us all huddle closer.

"This story is going to give you terminal goose bumps," she promised. "I heard it from a girl who made me swear not to tell anyone. She said the authorities didn't want it to get out."

"But it's all right to tell us?" I said anxiously.

"Of course, you're my mates," said Frankie. "And I'm going to tell it exactly how she told it to me."

Kenny's eyes gleamed and Lyndz's looked as if they were going to pop right out of her head. I gulped. Frankie's the best teller of scary tales I know. Outside, a cloud had gone across the sun, and the hall suddenly became full of eerie, flitting shadows.

"It happened at Gawdy Castle exactly three years ago," Frankie began. "In fact, by a very weird coincidence, it happened three years to the day this Friday!"

Lyndz drew in her breath. "That's the day we're going!"

"I know. That's why we'd better all be careful, because the terrible events I'm about to describe could well happen to any one of us."

Frankie was really enjoying putting the frighteners on us, but we were all loving it. "Not one word of what I am going to tell you can go outside this group," she said commandingly. "Do you swear?"

I heard Kenny mutter, "Get on with it, Spaceman." But the rest of us just nodded frantically.

"Then I'll begin," said Frankie in her special storytelling voice. "It was the day of the school safari trip and the weatherman had forecast storms. The skies were darkening as the school coach drove through the gates of Gawdy Castle. But no one wanted to miss out on seeing the animals, so the castle rangers decided to risk taking the children out in the Landrovers. They thought the storm would hold off."

"But it didn't," whispered Lyndz.

"No, it didn't. It began thundering and lightning like the end of the world. Soon rain was coming down so heavily it was impossible to see out of the windscreen. The rangers cut the tour short and told the children and teachers to shelter in the old castle. Now there was one boy, whose name was Peter Harris..."

"I've heard of him," said Kenny.

"Can I PLEASE tell my story without anyone interrupting?"

We all tried not to giggle at Frankie's impression of Mrs Weaver.

"Well, anyway, Peter soon got bored with looking at pictures of dead dukes and duchesses. And though the suits of armour were quite interesting, what he really wanted to see were the medieval torture chambers in the dungeons."

"Dun dun du-un!" interrupted a sarky voice.

Emma Hughes was smiling down at us. I say "smile". It was more like the lipless grin you see on mummies.

"Bug off, Emma," said Frankie.

"Oh, I'm SO sorry," said Emma in a scornful voice. "Was I interrupting your little storytelling session, Frankie? Why don't I finish it for you? Let me see. Oh, yes." Emma put on a fake scary voice. "Peter goes down into the dungeon where the ghost of a tortured prisoner jumps out at him, going 'Whooo!', and drags poor little Peter right inside the wall. When he fails to return to the minibus, the teachers and other kids search the castle for him. They search for over an hour. They've almost given up when Peter suddenly reappears in the main hall. But he's not the same normal, happy boy who left home that morning. His hair and eyebrows have turned snow white and he can't talk. He can only mumble like a great big baby…" Emma's voice had dropped to a whisper.

"That's horrible," said Lyndz in a trembly voice.

Emma gave a spiteful laugh. "And not one word of it is true! My brother played football with Peter Harris only the other day. That stupid ghost story's been going round for years. I can't believe Frankie swallowed it!"

CHAPTER TWO

It took the combined strength of the rest of the Sleepover Club to stop an enraged Frankie throwing herself at Emma.

"Where's the other Queen of Darkness today?" panted Kenny, still hanging on to a furious Frankie.

"Yeah, you want to be careful," said Lyndz. "If I was you, I wouldn't want to get Frankie angry without my evil twin for back-up."

As everybody in the village knows, Emma Hughes and Emily Berryman, aka the M&Ms, are our deadly enemies. This was one of the few times I'd ever seen one without the other.

Without her snooty bodyguard, Emma looked strangely incomplete.

"If you must know," she said stiffly, "Emily's caught—" She glanced around to make sure no one was listening and dropped her voice, "—erm, nits."

Kenz totally cracked up. "Oh, that's made my day! Emily Berryman's got head lice!! Can't you just imagine her scratching herself like a monkey!"

"My sympathy's with the nits personally," Frankie growled, still trying to wriggle free.

"Aren't you scared you'll catch them, Emma?" said Lyndz wickedly. "You've always got your heads together plotting some little scheme. Her evil creepy-crawlies wouldn't have far to jump."

Kenny gave a fake gasp. "Yikes, Emma!! I just saw something crawl into your hair! Dad says nits LURVE clean, blonde hair. He says that's like head lice heaven to them."

Kenny's dad is a doctor. Kenz says this is why she revels in blood and gore and all things icky. We don't totally buy this. We just think she's bizarre!

Emma was furious with Kenny. "You don't think I'd fall for that old trick, do you?" she spat. She stuck her nose in the air, obviously meaning to flounce away.

At that moment we all noticed the pretty blonde girl standing behind her.

"Hi, Emma, they said I'd find you in here!" she beamed. "Your mum fixed everything. Mrs Poole says I can come into school with you any time I'm at a loose end."

It was blatantly obvious Emma hadn't expected to see her friend in the dinner hall. "Oh, that's erm, super!" she gushed. "Why don't I show you round the school?" And she practically dragged the mystery girl towards the door.

"That's them, isn't it?" I heard the girl say excitedly. "They're just like you described, Emma! But it sounded like you were having an argument."

She's Australian, I thought. The new girl had exactly the same accent as Brad Martin, our favourite Aussie soap star.

I saw panic flicker over Emma's face. She gave a nervous giggle. "Oh, we're always kidding around like that. It doesn't mean anything."

I thought I must have misheard. It was quite possible. By this time Frankie had worked herself into a major razz.

"...plus I hope that hideous ghost drags her into a wall and they never EVER find her body!" she finished up breathlessly.

I was horrified. "Frankie, don't say that! Suppose Emma got ghost-napped for real. How would you feel then?"

"I'd think she deserves all she gets," Frankie said spitefully.

"Yeah, if the ghost wants her, let it have her," said Kenz.

"I agree," said Lyndz. "What do you reckon, Rosie-posie?"

Rosie jumped. "Oh, sorry, I was miles away."

"Must have been somewhere depressing," said Kenz cheerfully. "You looked gutted just then."

Rosie looked anxious. "I didn't, did I? Well, I'm fine, honestly."

She wasn't but we didn't find that out till later.

Frankie spent the rest of the afternoon dreaming up ways for us to avenge ourselves on Emma Hughes. By home time, she'd narrowed it down to three personal faves.

1. Pouring cold baked beans over Emma's head.

2. Smuggling fresh droppings from the school rabbit into her lunch box.

3. Stuffing old, v. smelly cream cheese in our enemy's P.E. shoes.

"I vote for the beans," giggled Lyndz.

Kenny shook her head. "Uh-uh. Rabbit droppings have better shock-value."

"Yeah," said Frankie. "Plus Emma's shoes are bound to be naturally cheesy anyway!"

Everyone fell about. Everyone but Rosie, that is.

I couldn't help noticing that our mate didn't join in Frankie's scheming. She'd been quiet all day. Any time we asked what was wrong, she said she had a headache.

This is typical Rosie. She keeps her worries so bottled up, Kenny says it's a wonder steam doesn't spurt from her ears. She's heaps more chilled than she was when she first moved to

Cuddington though. It used to take weeks before she'd admit anything was bothering her. Now it's days at most. Though even now, she tends to withdraw inside herself at the first sign of trouble.

I couldn't help feeling tense as we walked home. Mum says I have to learn not to be so sensitive. But I can't bear those jangly vibes when people are upset, can you? Suddenly I noticed something totally unbelievable. Emma and her new friend were following us.

The others noticed it at exactly the same moment.

Emma was obviously desperate for us not to notice her. Each time one of us looked back, she bent down and pretended to tie her shoelace, which has to be the most pathetic ruse ever. (Kenny reckoned she must have seen it on an old 1970s cop show!) Emma's friend was obviously wondering what on earth was going on.

"I've had enough of this," growled Frankie. "No one spies on the Sleepover Club and gets away with it."

"Spying?" I said in surprise. "Why would Emma spy on us?"

"Because she's gone over to the dark side, dummy," said Frankie. She blocked the pavement, very obviously waiting for the two girls to catch us up. "What's going on?" she called to them in an aggressive voice. "You've been sticking to us like fly paper all day."

Emma went bright red, but to my astonishment, the new girl beamed at Frankie and stuck out her hand. "Hi, you must be Frankie!" she said in a genuinely friendly voice. "I can tell from your gorgeous curly hair. Emma's told me all about you guys. I'm Kirstin."

Frankie looked totally confused. She just did NOT know how to react. I felt it was down to me to jump in and save my fellow blonde from humiliation. I grabbed Kirstin's hand and pumped it up and down.

"Hi, I'm Fliss. Let me introduce the others. From left to right: Rosie, Lyndz, Kenny and yes, the one with her mouth open is Frankie. I just lurve your trainers, by the way."

Kirstin looked pleased. "I got them in Sydney, just before we flew over. I'm Australian if you hadn't guessed." She pronounced it "guissed".

"I thought so! She sounds exactly like the characters in *South Beach*, doesn't she?" Lyndz said excitedly.

"Emma told me you guys had a bit of a *South Beach* craze going. I heard you met Brad Martin." Kirstin made a flirty face. "That guy is so dishy!!"

"Emma TOLD you we met Brad?" Frankie said suspiciously.

"She said she almost fainted when he invited you guys up on stage."

Frankie scowled. "She must have fainted from jealousy. It was us he invited to perform with him, not the Gruesome Two—"

Emma frantically tried to shut her up. "So, you've finally met my e-pal," she interrupted brightly. "We've been e-mailing each other for over a year now." Emma went into peals of fake laughter. "But you knew that already, silly me! I'm always telling you about Kirstin, aren't I?"

"You are?" said Kenny.

Emma Hughes suddenly looked at her watch. "Heavens!" she said in an artificial voice. "Is that the time! We're going to be SO late for my grandmother's party." She flashed us a strangely pleading smile. "See you later, guys!"

Before we could say "Huh?" Emma dragged her bewildered e-pal up the road and out of sight.

Frankie stared after them with a puzzled expression. "Did you hear that, or did I imagine it?"

"What?" we chorused.

Frankie gulped noisily. "I thought she said, 'See you later, guys'."

Kenny looked thoughtful. "She did say that, actually."

"Is it a crime?" I said timidly.

Frankie looked outraged. "It is, actually, Felicity Proudlove. A crime against Nature. Emma made it sound like we were friends with her!"

Kenny shuddered. "That is creepy."

"She was weird at dinner time too," said Lyndz.

"Maybe she really has got nits or ants in her pants or whatever?" Rosie suggested.

"Bats in her belfry more like," Kenz sniggered.

Frankie shook her head. "Emma's up to something. But she won't get away with it. I'm going to be watching her very closely."

"Listen to Frankie the super spy!" Lyndz giggled.

I was feeling slightly hurt. Why did Frankie have to draw attention to my name like that? It's not my fault my new stepdad is called Andy Proudlove. Mind you, my real dad's name is even worse. It's Sidebotham, would you believe. When it comes to names, my family has the worst luck.

"Mum will be worrying," I sighed. "I'll see you guys tomorrow."

I waved to my mates and went speeding down the street. I was still waiting at the pelican crossing when I heard Rosie call my name. She caught me up breathlessly. "Have you got a sec? I need to talk to you."

I had an awful feeling like going down too fast in a lift. Rosie can be really touchy sometimes. Obviously I'd upset her and that's why she'd been acting so strangely. I decided to get in first.

"I don't know what I've done, Rosie, but I'm so SO sorry. I'll make it up to you, I promise. And what's more I'll never ever do it again, erm, whatever it was."

Rosie looked confused. "What? No, Fliss, you haven't done anything. But I'm really worried about something and I need to talk to someone."

A warm glow started up inside me. Rosie trusted me. "You can tell me anything, dummy," I said. "I'm your mate."

I stood at the crossing for ten minutes, listening to Rosie.

When I finally walked up my front path and put the key in the door, I barely heard my brother and sister's wails. I trudged upstairs to my bedroom, shut the door, and collapsed miserably on to my bed.

We'd been looking forward to this trip for ever: since Kenny's sister Molly went to the same safari park. We'd daydreamed about what animals we'd see and what outfits we'd wear. We'd planned in detail the wonderful sleepover feast we'd have afterwards.

Now our dreams had ended up in the dustbin of disappointments.

I knew the awful truth behind Rosie's headaches.

She couldn't afford to come. Her dad was supposed to send the money but he'd forgotten and now he'd gone away on business. Rosie's mum was sorry, but she didn't have any cash to spare.

I was so upset, I felt as if my insides had been put into an ice-cream maker and churned into a great big, multicoloured mess.

What was I going to do? I didn't have enough money to pay for Rosie. I couldn't even ask anyone for help. She had totally sworn me to secrecy.

That meant Rosie was relying on me to come up with a plan to save the big Sleepover Safari. I really hoped I wouldn't let her down.

CHAPTER THREE

Morning came and I still hadn't come up with a solution.

To make matters worse my fringe totally would NOT lie down. "Oh, well," I told my reflection unhappily. "Looks like you'll be spending the day looking like a scruffy blonde cockatoo."

When I went downstairs, I discovered Mum had woken me up half an hour later than usual. So it was one mad dash to bolt down my Crispy Loops and sprint to the car.

To make my day even more depressing, Joe and Hannah screamed in their car seats all the way to school. Did I mention they look exactly like my stepdad? Don't laugh, it's true! Andy has absolutely no waistline and only a very, very small amount of fine, tufty hair. Don't get me wrong. I'm crazy about Andy. I tell my mates he's the best stepdad in captivity. But I'm not crazy about being trapped in a small car with two roaring, miniature, Andy look-alikes. Not to mention my brother Callum who was whingeing about this stupid game he'd seen on kids' MTV.

By the time Mum dropped me off, I'd gone deaf in both ears. I'm not exaggerating. I couldn't even hear the bell. I was also humungously late. By the time I stumbled into my classroom Mrs Weaver was reading out the last name on the register. It was awful. The entire class turned to stare at me.

I sheepishly took my seat. Rosie whispered, "Any ideas yet?"

I shook my head. "Not yet."

In my embarrassment, I'd completely forgotten my Rosie dilemma, but now it came flooding back.

Rosie deserves to go on this safari more than anyone, I thought fiercely. Life is rough for her at times. Her dad walked out on them some time ago and since then he hasn't really showed much interest in her and Tiffany. He makes slightly more effort with her brother Adam, who has cerebral palsy. But Rosie says it's like he thinks she doesn't need him or something. Luckily Rosie's mum copes brilliantly, but sometimes money is tight.

I'd feel terrible if we had to go without her. But I still had no idea how to help. Suddenly I realised that the entire class was looking in my direction.

"What do you think, Felicity?"

Mrs Weaver's voice sounded deceptively kind. Unfortunately I had no idea what she'd just said.

"Urmm, could you please repeat the question?"

Mrs Weaver narrowed her eyes into two scary laser beams. "Weren't you listening, dear?"

This was a toughie. Frankie would have no problem telling a little white lie. But this is me we're talking about and I am physically incapable of being dishonest. Take my promise to Rosie. I'd never break her confidence, even if I was threatened with hideous torture. That's the way I am.

So I was forced to stammer out the truth. "No, s-sorry, Mrs Weaver. I wasn't listening. It won't happen again."

I didn't think Frankie would ever let me live it down. She mimicked me all through break. "Sorry, Mrs Weaver, it won't happen again," she said in a breathy little voice. "Fliss, you're SUCH a wuss!"

Lyndz thought Frankie's impression was brilliant. She shrieked with laughter until – you guessed it – she got one of her famous attacks of hiccups. Usually I flap around like a mother hen, suggesting every cure in the *Bible of Hiccups*. But this morning I had absolutely no sympathy. Lyndz shouldn't have been laughing at me in the first place.

"Frankie, will you leave Fliss alone? It's getting boring now!"

It was Rosie's turn to do an impression, a scarily accurate one of her bossy big sister, Tiffany.

Frankie scowled. "Kenny thinks it's funny, don't you, Kenz?"

"The first few times I did," Kenny said truthfully. "Now it's kind of annoying."

At that moment a shadow fell over us. We looked up to see Emma with her pointy nose stuck in the air.

"Oh, it's you," Frankie sniffed. "Thought I could smell something."

Lyndz giggled, then hiccuped loudly.

"Where's your e-pal today?" I asked Emma.

"Her parents took her to London to do some sightseeing."

It was weird. Emma must have known we wanted her to go away, but for some reason she just went on standing there, looking incredibly uncomfortable.

If you'd taken a photograph at that moment, we'd have probably looked like we were all playing a peculiar game of musical statues.

"Is there anything you want, Emma?" Frankie asked sweetly. "Like a nice empty coffin to crawl into?"

Emma always looks really stressed. This is partly her hairstyle. She pulls her ponytail so tight, it literally makes her eyes bulge. But I've never seen her look so scared before.

"I just, erm, wanted to let you know that Kirstin's coming with us to Gawdy Castle on Friday," she mumbled.

Frankie shrugged. "Are we supposed to jump up and down?"

"No, I just thought you might—"

For a minute I thought Emma was going to burst into tears in front of us. She pulled herself together and tried again. "The thing is, Kirstin seems to think you guys are fun, so I was wondering if..." Emma couldn't quite bring herself to finish her sentence.

"Yes, your nose is too big," Kenny sniggered. "Oh, sorry, Emma, that is what you were wondering, isn't it?"

"Ha ha! Very funny." Emma was just plain angry now. "I didn't want to ask you losers in the first place. It's Kirstin who wanted me to." With that, she stormed off.

This might sound disloyal, but I couldn't help feeling sorry for Emma. I know how it feels when your best friends are off school. One time there was this nasty bug going around. Absolutely everyone caught it, except for me. Frankie, Rosie, Kenny and Lyndz were all off school for three whole days. I still remember how I felt sitting by myself in the dining hall. Every night I prayed to catch that bug. At least then I'd have some teeny-weeny microbes for company.

Being ill is horrible but loneliness is much, much worse. Emma obviously felt so exposed and vulnerable without Emily that she was even prepared to risk total humiliation by talking to us.

Kenny looked baffled. "The poison dwarf was acting well weird."

Lyndz had a listening expression. "Good, they've gone finally." Her hiccups, she meant. "So what do you think Emma was going on about?"

"You don't think she's just trying to be friendly?" I suggested.

Frankie knocked on my skull. "Are you feeling OK, Flissie?"

"She could have changed," I said nervously. "People do."

The others stared at me then went into complete hysterics.

"They do," I protested. But my friends refused to take me seriously.

On the way home, Rosie and I lagged behind the others.

"I'm a useless friend," I told her miserably. "I've been racking my brains, but I still can't think of anything."

Rosie tried to smile. "Thanks for trying, Flissie. Just promise not to tell the others. I'd hate them feeling sorry for me."

"I won't," I told her earnestly. "But for what it's worth, I don't think they would pity you. They'd want to help."

Rosie shook her head. "I'm not a charity case. It's bad timing, that's all. Mum had to fork out for new equipment for Adam. I can't exactly begrudge him that."

I gave her shoulder a squeeze. "Of course you can't. But we're your friends, Rosie-posie. You'd help us, if it was the other way round. I think you should give them a chance."

I could tell she wasn't convinced and decided I had to try harder.

"Remember that time Mrs Weaver said my project on the Ancient Romans needed more work? I had just about killed myself drawing those togas. I was gutted. And what did you guys do to cheer me up?"

"We baked you a batch of our special, best friend, triple chocolate chip cookies," Rosie mumbled.

"You see!" I told her.

"It's not the same. I can't expect you guys to pay for my school trip. How embarrassing would that be?" Her voice was gritty with despair.

"We couldn't give you all the money anyway. I worked it out last night. Even if we all chipped in our pocket money, we'd still be exactly seven pounds and fifty pence short. But I could ask my mum..."

Rosie looked horrified. "Flissie, no! Don't even think about doing that! Mum would feel humiliated."

"OK, OK. Stupid idea," I said hastily. "Look, relax. We'll figure it out somehow."

Rosie blew her nose. "Thanks, Flissie you're a really special friend."

It's nice when someone tells you you're special, but I felt I had to tell her the truth.

"We're all your friends, Rosie. And I still think you should tell the others. They're going to be SO hurt when they realise," I added sneakily.

That evening the twins seemed to be screaming non-stop so I took myself off for a soothing early night. I put on my favourite cosy PJs that Mum got from Miss Selfridge. The top has this sweet Pink Panther motif. Then I snuggled up in bed, reading the stars in my magazine. This probably sounds dumb, but I don't just read what they write for my birth sign, Virgo. I read the star signs for all my mates. Frankie's Aries. Her stars said she was feeling reckless but she should learn to look before she leaps. I turned to Rosie's birthday, but by this time I was having trouble concentrating. The screams seemed to be getting louder, in fact they were worryingly close. My door opened and Andy appeared with a screaming baby under one arm and our phone in his free hand. "It's Frankie," he told me. "She says it's urgent."

I took the phone and Andy tactfully went out and closed the door.

"Is something wrong?" I gulped.

Frankie sounded incredibly serious. "I'll say. The Sleepover Club's got a crisis on its hands. I don't know how to break it to you, Flissie, so I'll just say it straight."

Frankie might be a drama queen, but she only uses that tone of voice when something's really, really wrong. I squinched my eyes tight shut, and waited for her to give me the bad news. I didn't know for sure what Frankie was going to say, but I could guess. Obviously my wimpy ways had alienated my mates so totally that they no longer wanted to be friends.

"Are you listening?" Frankie sounded just like our teacher.

I nodded miserably.

She sighed. "You do know I can't see you on the phone?"

Luckily Frankie couldn't see me blush either. "Sorry. I mean, yes, I'm ready," I told her bravely.

"You'd better sit down. Rosie can't afford to come on the safari!"

I am SO selfish! In the last few seconds, I'd

flashed through a zillion awful scenarios, all of them ending with me being left with no mates. The Rosie situation had totally slipped my mind!

"Aren't you shocked?" Frankie prompted.

No, I was confused, that's what I was. First because – hurray! – my sleepover mates were still speaking to me. But mostly because I couldn't begin to imagine how Frankie had found out Rosie's secret.

"SAY something, you wally!" said Frankie impatiently.

"Ermm..."

Frankie began to chuckle. "It's all right, you dippy duck. Rosie said she told you. I have NO idea how you persuaded her to 'fess up, but you did a wicked job."

I felt myself go weak with relief. "I did?"

"But seriously, what are we going to do? Even if we gave her all our pocket money, we'd still be..."

"...seven pounds and fifty pence short." I finished Frankie's sentence for her.

"Exactly. And she's forbidden us to ask our parents."

I yawned. "Can we talk about this at school?

The twins are screaming so hard I can't hear myself think. Plus I'm really tired."

Frankie giggled. "Poor Flissie, you should get some earplugs. See you tomorrow then. Sleep tight, don't let the bugs bite."

We hadn't solved Rosie's problem, but as I climbed back into bed, I felt a weight lifting off my shoulders. I was still worried about my friend, but at least I didn't have to come up with a solution on my own.

Next morning at break, we met up in a corner of the cloakroom that teachers tend not to check. Probably because it's so smelly. I'm not exaggerating: it reeks of gym shoes and boys' socks. But this was a serious Sleepover Club emergency, so I bravely breathed through my mouth.

"Anyone got any good ideas?" Kenny demanded.

We all shook our heads.

"Sorry, guys," Rosie mumbled.

"Stop apologising!" Frankie told her. "We're the Sleepover Club, right? There's no way any of us is missing out on that safari."

"But I don't see what you can do." Rosie sounded as if she'd given up hope. "Mum hasn't got the money and that's that."

"I could help you." A pink-looking Kirstin slipped out from behind the coats. "I wasn't snooping," she explained. "I just couldn't help overhearing."

Frankie's eyes blazed with anger. "Did Emma put you up to this? I think it's disgusting of you to eavesdrop on our conversation."

Kirstin looked shocked. "Emma wouldn't do anything like that. She's crazy about you all. Every time she e-mails, she tells me the goss about you guys and all about the latest mad sleepover you had together."

Frankie stared at her. "You mean like, a sleepover with us and Emma?"

"A sleepover with Emma and US?" Lyndz echoed.

"All of us together?" Kenny croaked.

"Under the same roof?" I added.

Kirstin giggled. "You Poms have a weird sense of humour, you know that? But I was trying to be serious. I'd really like to help you, Rosie, if you'll let me. My olds always give me way too much spending money. I'd like you to have it." She smiled at Frankie. "I heard what you said and I know Emma would agree with you. You Sleepover girls should stick together."

The bell rang to signal end of break.

"Promise me you'll think about it?" Kirstin asked Rosie. She swung her bag over her shoulder and went sprinting off to class.

"Help!" said Frankie in a strangled voice. "Tell me we didn't have that incredibly disturbing conversation."

We stared after Kirstin. With her healthy suntan and sunkissed blonde hair, she really did look exactly like a character from *South Beach*. But what on *earth* had Emma been telling her?

CHAPTER FOUR

"Aaargh!" screamed Frankie. "Aaargh!!!!"

I couldn't blame her for letting off steam. We'd been controlling ourselves heroically for HOURS. First we had to suffer all the way through double maths, then we were forced to share our dinner table with two tragic boys from Mr Pownall's class. One of them had a massive bogey hanging out of his nose, which totally put us off our food.

Now we were huddled in a windy but happily bogey-free corner of the playground, trying to figure out what in the world was going on.

"It just doesn't make sense," wailed Frankie. "This situation is doing my head in. Emma and Emily HATE us. They always have and they always will. It's like, a cosmic law!"

"So why would Emma tell someone she was a member of the Sleepover Club, when she totally despises us?" Lyndz pondered.

"A girl on totally the other side of the world," I added.

Rosie was crumbling her sandwich into teeny-weeny pieces.

"Earth to Rosie," Kenny teased. "You must be happy at any rate. It was well cool of Kirstin to offer you that dosh."

Rosie looked more depressed than ever. "I can't take it. Mum would hate me to take charity from a stranger."

Frankie's mouth fell open. "Rosie Cartwright, I can't believe you said that. This is your big miracle! You don't turn miracles down!"

"Yeah, how else are we going to get you to Gawdy Park?" said Kenny.

"You won't let us ask our parents," Lyndz pointed out.

"I can't help it, it wouldn't be right," said poor Rosie.

Frankie scowled. "I don't think you really want to go, or you wouldn't give up so easily."

I quickly put my arm round Rosie. "Of course she does, don't you? You want to see lions and tigers, don't you?"

"And the monkeys. Don't forget the sweet little monkeys, Rosie-posie," Lyndz said temptingly.

Rosie was torn between laughing and crying. "I'm not four, you know! Of course I want to come, you idiots!"

"Then take Kirstin's cash and come!" Lyndz moaned. "The suspense is totally killing us."

Rosie took a deep breath. "OK, I'll do it."

We stared at her. "Seriously? You're REALLY coming?" I squeaked.

"Too right," she said fiercely. "This is my miracle, like Frankie says. I'll go and tell Kirstin now."

Frankie punched the air. "Hallelujah! Rosie Cartwright has finally seen the light!"

"Erm, I don't want to be negative," said Kenny.

"Then don't," said Frankie rudely.

Kenny looked genuinely worried. "What's Rosie going to tell her mum, about suddenly finding the money for the trip?" she asked.

"I never thought of that," Frankie admitted.

"Bums! We're such idiots," groaned Lyndz.

"Then that's it," Rosie whispered. "That was my last chance."

"Sorry, Rosie," said Kenny humbly. "I didn't mean to ruin your miracle."

"We could try to dream up a really good story," Frankie suggested.

"I can't lie," I told them. "You know I can't. I totally go to pieces."

"She's hopeless," Kenny agreed.

Frankie went unusually quiet and I could see her racking her brains. "All right," she said at last. "Now you'd better brace yourselves. This is really going to shock you, and you'll probably never hear me say this again, but I think it's time we asked one of our parents for advice."

Lyndz almost fell over. "Advice! Are you crazy?"

To my surprise Kenny said, "She's right. The question is which parent? You know how weird grown-ups can get about money."

"We could ask Fliss's mum," Lyndz suggested. "She's pretty chilled these days."

Kenny beamed. "That's true, she is! What do you guys think?"

Everyone agreed, even Rosie. My mum has really mellowed since the twins were born but even so I was chuffed that my mates were willing to trust her with this incredibly delicate situation.

After school I ran ahead to make sure there were no icky, used Pampers lying around. The twins were still napping luckily. Mum was in the kitchen catching up on chores before the round of feeding and changing started all over again.

She looked touched when I said we needed her advice. "I bet you girls could do with a snack too," she beamed.

My mates came in through the back door, on cue. "There's some leftover trifle, if you girls want some?" Mum told them. "Hope you don't mind if I get on with peeling these potatoes?"

That's another change I have to thank the twins for. Ever since Mum had the babies, dieting's gone right out the window! She says salads don't give her the stamina she needs to run around after four children.

"I'll help," Rosie told my mum shyly. "I'm a dynamite spud peeler."

While Mum and Rosie got busy, I dished up trifle for everyone.

"Should I save some for Callum?" I called to Mum.

She shook her head. "He's at his friend's. James's mum gives them treats galore."

We quickly got stuck into our bowls of raspberry trifle. Frankie, the messiest ten year old in the entire world, ended up with a major whipped-cream moustache and lurid, raspberry-pink lips.

"You look like a mad clown!" Lyndz giggled.

"Yeah?" said Frankie. "Well you've got custard in your eyelashes, so there!"

My mum wiped her hands on a towel. "The twins will want their tea in ten minutes. So if you're serious about that advice, we haven't got long."

I could see Rosie going beetroot red with misery. "I've got myself in a real mess," she said, and poured out the whole story, up to the moment Emma's e-pal offered to give her the money for the trip.

Mum looked impressed. "She must like you."

"She doesn't even know me," said Rosie. "Kirstin only came over from Australia a few days ago. She doesn't know *any* of us."

"She doesn't know us, but she knows *of* us," Frankie explained, making it sound as clear as mud.

Mum laughed. "You're not telling me the Sleepover Club's reputation has spread to Australia?"

"Apparently it has," said Frankie, looking smug.

"I want to accept," said Rosie earnestly, "but I don't think it's right. What do you think, Mrs Proudlove?"

"I agree with you, Rosie," Mum said to everyone's disappointment. "You shouldn't take Kirstin's money. But don't worry, I'll give it to you."

Rosie started to protest.

"I'm not offering you a handout," Mum explained. "I'm offering you a business deal. Come over on Saturday and bake some of your gorgeous cookies. I'll provide the ingredients, but you'll be providing the labour. I want six batches so I can put some in the freezer. Callum and Andy adored the cookies you made for Fliss. You'd be doing me a big favour."

"I would?" Rosie's bottom lip quivered.

"Yes, you would," said Mum firmly. "Is it a deal?"

"YES, YES, YES!!" yelped Frankie, going right over the top as usual. "She accepts, don't you, Rosie-posie?"

Rosie was blinking back tears furiously. "OK, Mrs Proudlove," she said when she could make her voice work. "It's a deal."

We all dived on Rosie, hugging her and messing up her hair. I was so happy I can't tell you. Plus I was incredibly grateful to my mum for solving Rosie's problem so brilliantly.

"I'll call your mother and explain that you'll be doing some chores for me on Saturday morning," said Mum.

"But Rosie will be here already," Lyndz giggled. "We all will."

Mum looked blank. "Oh, yes, of course she will!" she said hastily.

I wagged my finger. "You forgot it was my turn to hold a sleepover, didn't you?"

She looked embarrassed. "Actually I did. Look, you girls are always welcome, you know that. But small babies tend to disturb everyone's sleep, and unusual comings and goings disturb small babies."

I swallowed. Was Mum saying we had to cancel our safari sleepover?

"Suppose you had your sleepover in the lounge," she suggested. "Would that be OK, girls?"

I brightened. "Excellent!"

"We could borrow a tent from Lyndz's brothers," said Frankie at once, "and pretend we're on a proper African safari."

This idea got us completely overexcited.

I was still buzzing as I was getting into bed. Everything was coming together. I even knew what my safari outfit was going to look like. Do you want to know? I planned to be wearing dark blue jeans with turn-ups, a pink t-shirt with a cartoon monkey on it and my favourite baby pink and blue trainers. Stylish or what!

I stretched out in my lovely comfy bed. Aaah! I could finally relax. Thanks to Mum's creative problem solving, my mates were going to have a fabulous Safari Sleepover to remember.

CHAPTER FIVE

Thursday morning got off to a brilliant start. I'd packed my school bag the night before, so I didn't have the usual last-minute rush to find my pencil case and reading book. My shoes were polished. My clothes were washed and pressed and my ponytail had gone just right. My mates think I'm crazy to bother about stuff like that, but Mum always says, "If you look good on the outside, Fliss, you'll feel better on the inside!" And I think that's true.

"You're looking chuffed with yourself," Frankie whispered from behind as Mrs Weaver took the register.

"I'm just so excited about tomorrow," I hissed back.

Rosie was visibly glowing with happiness. "Me too," she mouthed.

Mrs Weaver was handing out tourist brochures with important info on Gawdy Castle Safari Park. On the cover was a picture of a full-grown lioness sprawling in the long grass with her cubs.

At first the boys acted like they were way too cool to even take an interest. Then they really got into it, swapping gory tales about man-eating tigers and reading out wildlife statistics. Boys are obsessed with world records, aren't they? Even Ryan was raving on about the biggest this and the smallest that, and you'd think he'd have more sense.

Personally I didn't care if something was the biggest or the smallest or even the most inbetweenest, I just wanted to see these gorgeous animals roaming in the wild. It would be the next best thing to visiting Africa or India or wherever. (Don't tell the others, but I was a teensy bit hazy about where tigers actually come from.)

When Mrs Weaver told us that the forecast for Friday was sunshine and blue skies, I turned to give Frankie and Lyndz a big thumbs up.

That's when I caught sight of Emma. She was staring blankly out of the window, ignoring her booklet, not taking part in the general safari park fever. Suddenly Emma sensed me watching. To my surprise she gave me a weak smile, then turned back to the window.

Things are getting way too weird round here, I thought. I couldn't understand why Emma was being so nice or why Kirstin was under the impression that her e-pal was a fully paid-up member of the Sleepover Club. But I was determined to get to the bottom of the mystery.

At break, while the others were playing a mad game of leapfrog on the field, I wandered off to find Emma.

She was sitting on the grass by herself, gloomily making a daisy chain. I checked I wasn't about to sit in anything gross then plunked myself down beside her.

"How's Emily doing?" I asked casually. "Any better?"

"Like you care," Emma said bleakly. "But that's OK. We don't like you guys either. You're always sniggering behind our backs."

Excuse me! I thought. Frankie and Kenny might snigger, but I have a very sweet little giggle, thank you very much. But I was trying to win Emma's confidence, so I just said, "What about Kirstin. Is she sightseeing again today?"

But Emma just jabbed her thumbnail viciously into a daisy stem and didn't reply.

"Look, I'm not stupid," I told her. "I know something's wrong. And I know it's got something to do with the Sleepover Club and Kirstin."

"Do you really want to know what's going on?" Emma said doubtfully.

"I said so, didn't I?"

"OK, I'll tell you. Kirstin lives right out in the Australian bush somewhere. She doesn't even go to a proper school. She studies with the Air School or something."

"Kirstin has flying lessons?" I gasped.

Emma gave a weary sigh. "Fliss, honestly,"

she said in her prissy voice. "The Air School is when they teach you on the radio and the Internet and whatever. The point is, she lives in the middle of nowhere, but she's got all these friends, don't ask me how. Every time she sent me an e-mail, she seemed to be having such a great time. I didn't have anything to write about, except feuding with you guys, and getting my homework in on time. Again. So, well, I did this stupid thing—"

"What did you do?" I couldn't imagine what Emma had done that could be so bad.

"I pretended you were my friends," Emma said miserably. "I even told her you had sleepovers at my house."

I didn't know what to say.

She glared at me. "Well, go on! Run back and tell your little friends. Then you can all crack jokes about how pathetic I am."

But I didn't feel like joking. I didn't even feel like smiling. I'd never heard anything so sad in my life.

"But why did you pick us if you hate us so much?" I blurted out.

Emma looked at me as if I was dense. "Don't you get it? You guys have it all. You look so good for a start. You're totally up to date. Even Kenny and she doesn't even care about fashion."

Boy, we must be cool, I thought. Even our enemies think we're stylish.

Emma was still ticking off our positive qualities.

"Frankie is just so original. Plus she has a mad sense of humour. Kenny is ace at football. Let's face it, she's better than the boys."

"That's true," I agreed.

"Rosie is really sweet and loyal. Lyndz is so good with animals, she's like Cuddington's Doctor Dolittle or something," Emma's voice cracked. "So now you know. It was stupid, just a stupid fantasy. I never imagined that Kirstin would come to visit. Now she expects me to hang out with you all the time. I had to tell her we'd had a silly misunderstanding. I feel awful lying to her. But I don't know what to do!" Emma was furiously sniffing back tears.

I fished a clean tissue out of my pocket and gave it to Emma. "OK, Emma, blow your nose,"

I told her firmly. "I want you to listen carefully, because I just might have a plan."

By the time morning break was over, an outrageous alliance had been formed between the Sleepover Club and the non-nit-infested member of the M&Ms. Of course, when I say the Sleepover Club, I really mean me, Fliss. The others still had no idea of the scheme I was cooking up.

And as it turned out, I couldn't tell them until afternoon break. Cause Kenny had football practice at lunchtime. I shared out my family pack of Maltesers, then I dropped my bombshell.

My friends could not have looked more horrified if I'd grown a beard.

Frankie choked on her sweet. "Tell me you're joking," she said, when we'd finished banging her on the back.

I shook my head. "I'm not joking."

"NO WAY!" yelled Frankie. "I'm not pretending to be Emma's friend for one second, let alone an entire day."

Lyndz looked as furious as Frankie. "Fliss, this is the class trip we're talking about! We've been looking forward to it for aeons."

"I know," I said guiltily. "But—"

"But nothing. We can't enjoy ourselves with poisonous Emma tagging along."

"Kirstin will be there too," I pointed out. "Kirstin's way cool."

"You can invite Britney Spears for all I care," said Frankie sourly. "We still won't have a good time. I can't believe you've actually been fraternising with the enemy."

I felt terrible when Frankie put it like that, but I still thought I was right. "You didn't see her," I said miserably. "She looked so, I don't know, ashamed. I know if I was feeling that bad, one of you would try to help. But Emma's only got Emily."

There was a long silence.

"She does have a point," Kenny admitted.

"A very minor point," Frankie scowled.

"Imagine if the only person you could rely on was Emily," said Lyndz.

"Nightmare," shivered Kenny.

"And then Emily gets nits," I said.

"It wouldn't kill us to help Emma, would it?" Rosie asked.

"We could take a vote," suggested Lyndz.

"We don't need to vote." Frankie stood up.

Here we go, I thought drearily.

I almost fell over with shock when she said, "I say we help Emma out. No matter how smelly she is!" she added with an evil grin.

I stared at her. "Seriously?"

"Kirstin believes we're super cool. Let's keep it that way."

Frankie's change of heart took my breath away.

"We'll call it Operation Pretend Friend," suggested Rosie.

"Coo-ell," everyone giggled.

"So when does it start?" said Lyndz.

"O800 hours tomorrow." Frankie sounded like a soldier in a movie.

"It's not going to be easy," Lyndz warned.

"Yeah, we're constantly going to have to watch what we say." Kenny looked genuinely alarmed. "We don't actually have to be nice to Emma, do we?"

"Nice as pie," Frankie said sweetly. "Your face muscles will ache from all that fake smiling."

"It might be fun," said Rosie in a brave voice.

Kenny gave a yelp of laughter. "You sound like my mum when she's taking me to the dentist."

"At least dentists give you laughing gas," sighed Lyndz. "We've got to face Emma stone cold sober. What? What did I say?"

We'd gone into total hysterics. We kept trying to explain we weren't laughing at her, but that just sent us off into more mad hoots of laughter, and eventually Lyndz was laughing equally helplessly, though she had no idea what she was laughing at. We laughed until we were totally exhausted, then Kenny said weakly, "Oh, no! Stone cold sober!" And off we went again.

Thursday night is Mum's evening to go to her Keep Fit class and Andy and I were left in charge of the littlies. My stepdad is really easy to talk to, so I found myself telling him about Operation Pretend Friend, while I helped him bath the babies.

"Sounds dodgy to me," he said bluntly. "Lying has a nasty habit of getting out of control: 'Oh, what a tangled web we weave!' and all that."

"It's not really lying," I protested. "More like play acting. It's in a good cause."

"Sorry, princess, I don't think good can come out of lies. I really admire you though, for trying to help your little mate."

"But she's not my little mate," I wailed. "I HATE Emma. At least I used to. Now I'm just confused!"

"Here, put a nappy on him quick before anything leaks out," Andy commanded, passing me a very pink, clean Joe. He heaved an exasperated sigh. "Too late!"

When Joe and Hannah were finally tucked up in their little cots, Andy went to find Callum and tell him a story. It's the same one he tells my brother every night. Well, it's not exactly a story. Andy recites a long list of all the tools he uses on the building site, in a really peaceful, singsong voice, and eventually Callum goes glassy eyed and falls asleep.

I left Andy murmuring about hammers and pliers and escaped into the rosy pink privacy of my room. I was feeling abnormally stressed so I took my jumpers out of my wardrobe and refolded them really slowly, to calm myself down.

I hated to admit it but my down-to-earth stepdad had a point. I'd been so fixated on my rescue mission that I hadn't really thought about the consequences. I was trying to stop Emma getting hurt. But if the truth came out, someone else might get hurt – like Kirstin, or even me!

I suddenly felt sick. Suppose Andy was right and Operation Pretend Friend backfired? Our safari trip would be ruined. My mates would think it was my fault. What's more, they'd be right.

CHAPTER SIX

I made Andy recite that weird little rhyme about liars again the other day. It goes: 'Oh, what a tangled web we weave, when first we practise to deceive'. I don't know who wrote it, but boy, that guy totally knew what he was talking about!!

Our safari trip started out as a treat. But when the neighbourhood tweetie birds woke me at dawn on Friday, I felt like our class outing was suddenly looming over me like an especially threatening nightmare.

Complicated worries went round my brain. What if we let something slip and Kirstin found out what we were up to? She probably wouldn't realise we were trying to help Emma. She'd just think we were trying to make a fool of her! Omigosh, I thought, this trip is going to be harder work than school!!

I was so nervous that I was up and washed and dressed before the twins even made a squeak.

On the way to school Mum literally threatened to tie me to the roof-rack if I didn't calm down. "Calm DOWN, sweetie! You're not going to miss the coach."

"Mum, I'm totally calm!" I lied. "I'm just really excited. This is, like, the happiest day of my life."

I cowered behind the school gate and took a deep breath. I'm happy happy happy, I told myself bravely. I must look happy happy happy.

And like an actor bounding out of the wings, I ran into the playground, waving and smiling brightly.

My old sleepover mates were there already, chatting incredibly animatedly to our two new members. Kirstin was wearing cool casuals, just right for a day out, with a World Wildlife baseball cap perched on the back of her head. Poor Emma. She was proudly wearing a little top and combats, but they were in really eye-watering colours, like you only see on poisonous frogs. Plus she'd pulled her ponytail so tight it's a wonder it hadn't cut off her blood supply.

"Hi, guys," I gushed. "Are we totally excited or what?"

Frankie rolled her eyes at me. "Oh, we're beyond excited, Flissie. Way, way beyond."

Rosie nudged her. "Behave."

I gave Kirstin and Emma my most dazzling smile. "I was buzzing all night, weren't you? I couldn't sleep a wink."

"Oh, I know what you mean," said Emma at once.

"I slept like a log," Kirstin grinned. "But I went to Africa last summer, where we slept outdoors in all sorts of conditions. Plus we camp in the Australian outback loads. Safaris are always fun, wherever you have them."

Frankie was impressed. "You've been to Africa? You're only our age."

Kirstin pulled a face. "Mum and Dad are biologists. Right now we're living in the outback, but they're constantly dragging me all over the world."

"I wish my parents took me to exotic locations," Lyndz sighed.

"You wouldn't have time for sleepovers," Rosie pointed out.

"I would," Lyndz giggled. "I'd take you all with me, and we'd have a fabulous sleepover at the Taj Mahal."

"Now that IS a cool idea," laughed Kirstin.

Wow, I thought. It might have been sticky at first but Operation Pretend Friend was working. It was more than working. It was going like a dream!

"Where do you go to school?" Frankie was asking Kirstin.

"I don't," grinned Kirstin. "I just hook up to the School of the Air."

So it wasn't called the Air School after all. Know-all Emma didn't know as much as she liked to make out.

Mrs Weaver clapped her hands. "Quiet everyone. Yes, that includes you, Francesca."

Frankie was still chatting to Kirstin so she didn't hear. Lyndz smacked her bum with her baseball cap. Frankie swung round in surprise to see everyone looking at her. "Oops!" she giggled. "Looks like I pulled a Fliss. Sorry, Mrs Weaver. It's just that Kirstin's been on an actual safari in Africa. Plus she's being educated on the Internet."

Mrs Weaver was looking tired already and we weren't even on the coach yet. "Perhaps she'd like to tell us about it another time. Now I want you all to make an orderly line by the coach."

But Kenny had other ideas. "We've got to get the seat at the back," she hissed. She started elbowing her way to the front. Her aggressive tactics worked and we managed to bag the sacred back seat.

"Emma! Emma! You and Kirstin grab the seat in front of us," Frankie called. "Let's keep all the Sleepover Club girls together."

Emma forced a smile. "OK, Frankie, good idea!"

"Don't overdo it, Spaceman!" I told Frankie.

"I'm an actress," she said smugly. "I'm

playing the part of Emma's loyal sleepover buddy."

The coach started to move and everyone cheered.

"I really owe your mum," Rosie whispered in my ear. "I'd be missing this if it wasn't for her."

Kirstin and Emma were taking it in turns to read each other bits of historical info from their booklets. Kirstin was impressed that she was going to see a real castle. "You've got so much history in this country," she said.

"Aren't all you Australians descended from criminals?" Danny McCloud asked rudely, obviously hoping to get a rise out of her.

She laughed. "That's right! But you know what I'll never understand? You dozy Poms sent your criminals to live in paradise, and you all stayed home in the rain. How weird is that?"

Everyone thought this was hilarious.

"She told you, Danny!" Ryan grinned.

Kirstin winked at me and went back to reading about Gawdy Castle. I don't know how people can read in a coach, I don't actually like coaches that much. Especially at the back. It's well bumpy.

We were just halfway to the safari park when Martin Ainsley, this weedy new boy, threw up all over the boy who was sitting next to him.

Frankie clutched her nose. "That smells so-o rank!"

Kenny tried to see what was happening. "Urgh, it's got yellow lumps," she reported. "What on earth did Martin have for breakfast?"

"Don't be gross." I tried to pull her back on to her seat.

"I'm not gross. I'm taking a clinical interest. I'm going to be a doctor, remember?"

"Then maybe you should help clean it up," Frankie suggested.

I'm really brave about sick since Mum had the twins, but I was still relieved when we finally saw the sign for Gawdy Park.

We drove along beside a high stone wall for what seemed like miles. Behind the wall were tall trees, some just coming into leaf. At last, behind the trees, we saw the weathered battlements of an ancient castle.

"Yikes, is this castle haunted? It sure looks haunted to me," Kirstin said excitedly.

"It's really just an old museum," said Emma.

"Don't expect too much."

Kenny rolled her eyes. "The trouble with Emma is she's SO boring," she whispered.

"No imagination," Frankie agreed. "A ghost could walk right past her picking its nose and she wouldn't even notice."

We drove through the gates and pulled into the huge car park.

The only disadvantage about sitting at the back is that you're always last off. Plus Mrs Weaver slowed us down loads by making us listen to her long list of dos and don'ts. By the time we'd got out into the fresh air, Kenny was jiggling frantically up and down. "Oooh, I need a wee!"

"Have you seen the queue outside the loos?" Frankie moaned. "You'll be waiting for ever. Can't you hold on?"

"If you don't mind it coming out of my ears," Kenny said.

"I'm just worried you'll find this really boring," I heard Emma saying. "I mean you go to all these exciting places."

"Are you kidding!" said Kirstin. "Do you know how many fourteenth-century castles there are in Australia?" She made a zero with her finger and thumb.

"None?" guessed Emma.

"Exactly, none. This is a first for me."

"But no one lives in the castle any more," Emma said anxiously.

"You mean I won't actually see knights in armour! Shame!" Kirstin punched Emma's shoulder lightly. "Relax! Just being with you guys is the best treat."

But I thought Emma was right to warn Kirstin not to expect too much. I stared around in bewilderment. "So where are all the animals?"

Emma gave a snort of laughter. "You surely didn't expect to see them in the car park, you stupid—" She caught herself just in time. "I mean, you funny thing!" she said hastily.

I didn't take it too personally. Emma had been a member of the Sleepover Club for less than three hours. She'd been half of the Gruesome Twosome for years. Being spiteful was such a habit, I don't think she even knew she was doing it.

Kenny emerged from the loos at last and we all surged up the path to the massive gates

73

which separated the castle grounds from the actual safari park.

"It said in the booklet there's a maze in the grounds," said Kirstin excitedly. "I've always wanted to get lost in a maze."

Danny tapped his forehead. "Strange girl. She wants to get lost."

"You look worried," Rosie whispered in my ear.

"I was just wishing everyone could get along together," I whispered. "Like, why do we have to be Emma's pretend friends? Why can't we be her mates for real?"

Rosie smiled. "Even real mates don't get on ALL the time!"

"That's true," I agreed. "Remember that time we—"

Just then a ranger in jeans and an orange Gawdy Park body warmer came round the corner, closely followed by an elephant.

Everyone gasped. Obviously we'd all seen elephants on TV. But nothing compares with actually meeting one face to face. I don't know if you've ever seen an elephant close up, but they're MASSIVE. This one's legs were like small trees and it had more wrinkles than my grandma.

Then I started going, "Oh, oh, oh!" I was so overexcited, they were truly the only words I could get out.

Between the tree-trunk legs of the enormous elephant I'd spotted four small, tottery, grey feet. My friends saw them at exactly the same moment.

"It's got a baby!" I gasped. "Ohh, look at its darling ears!!"

"And that cute little trunk!" cooed Frankie.

"I want one!" said Lyndz.

"Don't be stupid, what would you do with a trunk?" Kenny teased.

"I meant I want a baby elephant, idiot," Lyndz told her.

"Watch her," I told Kirstin. "Lyndz kidnapped a baby pig one time."

"You never told me about that!" Kirstin said to Emma.

Emma blushed. "Didn't I?"

"She's probably used to Lyndz nicking animals, aren't you, Emma?" I said quickly. "She's a total klepto."

"I AM not," said Lyndz indignantly. "I'm a friend to Nature, that's what I am."

"Keep moving everyone!" Mrs Weaver told the class. "We've got an extremely tight schedule."

"Those gates are awesome," said Frankie as we finally stood waiting for the rangers to let us in.

"Why do they make them so big?" asked someone.

The park gates literally towered over us, making me feel like a little doll's house doll.

"They have to stop the animals getting out," Rosie said.

"What have they got in there? Dinosaurs?" asked Danny anxiously.

I felt excitement prickling in the pit of my stomach.

"In a few moments we'll be going on a tour of the safari park in the estate Landrovers. You must stay inside the Landrover unless the ranger tells you otherwise. Is that understood?"

Everyone nodded dutifully.

"You may not open the windows and you may certainly not lean out, Danny McCloud!"

Mrs Weaver said sharply. "You must follow the ranger's instructions at all times. Those are dangerous wild animals on the other side of those gates. They are not, repeat not, cuddly pets. In a few moments you'll meet the rangers who'll be taking us on our safari," Mrs Weaver explained. "After lunch we'll go on a tour of the castle and grounds."

"Excellent! Wonder what's for lunch?" said Kenny greedily.

Frankie went into victim mode. "I hope they've got stuff for vegetarians. It would be so-o unfair if they—"

But I never heard what Frankie thought would be so unfair, because at that moment the electric gates swung open and I heard the unmistakable, spine-tingling roar of a lion.

CHAPTER SEVEN

"Have you seen this humungous list of animals we're supposed to spot?" Frankie waved a sheet of paper in my face. "I can't BELIEVE how many types of animals there are. I think I'm going to fall off my bones with excitement if we see a lion!"

"That would be interesting," grinned Kenny. "I wonder what Frankie would actually look like with no bones?" she said to herself.

As you can tell, Kenny has the WEIRDEST mind.

We'd been on safari for twenty minutes, and so far the animals were keeping well out of our way. We tried to get ourselves in the right safari spirit but it's not easy when you're all squashed into a Gawdy Park Landrover.

When I say, "all" I mean all the Sleepover Club members, real and fake, plus, (GULP) Mrs Weaver. I know!! We weren't too thrilled about that either. We were really depressed when she insisted on coming with us.

"We'll look like teacher's pets," Frankie hissed.

"What's wrong with that?" Emma hissed back.

Kenny gave her a withering look. "You're actually a Martian, aren't you, Emma. But don't worry, you'll soon learn our earthling ways!"

Emma sucked in her breath but whatever she was going to say, she quickly thought better of it.

The Landrover went on bumping its way up a long, steep hill.

When we reached the top, the ranger stopped, so we could see Gawdy Park spread out below like a crumpled green and brown bedspread. Microscopic animals were moving around in the distance. I couldn't exactly see what they were, but they could have been cows and I would have still been amazed.

The ranger pointed out some deer grazing down by the river. "And you might just be able to make out a herd of elephants among those trees," he grinned.

"Why aren't those other elephants with them?" Lyndz asked him.

"The mum and baby? The littl'un got an infection and the vet wants to keep an eye on her."

"Poor thing!" gasped Lyndz. "I hope she'll be all right."

"I'm sure she'll be fine," said Mrs Weaver briskly. "So, Kirstin, is this anything like being on a real safari?"

We rolled our eyes at each other. Why are grown-ups so embarrassing? And how come they never know when they're in the way?"

Going downhill in a Landrover is even more uncomfortable than going up. Every time we went over a bump, our heads literally whacked the roof!

"Yikes!" Rosie squeaked suddenly.

"Did you hurt your head?" I said sympathetically.

She was pink with excitement. "No, I just saw a lion!"

The Landrover braked just in time for us to see the huge lion stroll past, barely a few metres from our window. Its shaggy gold mane was so long, it trailed in the dirt, like a rather bedraggled royal train. The lion seemed used to tourists. It just gave a bored yawn in our direction, exposing a mouth full of white, needle-sharp teeth.

Frankie gulped. "That's one kittykat I wouldn't want to play with."

"What a magnificent beast!" Emma said in her prissy voice.

Kenny nudged Frankie. "I thought you were going to fall off your bones if you saw a lion?"

"I'll make you fall off yours in a minute," Frankie told her.

Eventually the lion loped away and the Landrover continued chugging down the track. Five minutes later, the ranger stopped again, this time to let us watch some monkeys playing chase in the trees.

Monkeys are SO nosy. The instant they saw us they came swinging down from the branches, chattering to each other in shrill, annoyed-sounding voices. They landed on the top of the Landrover and peered in at the windows. One immediately started trying to remove the windscreen wipers. Another one chittered angrily at itself in one of the wing mirrors.

"Ugh, do they have to show us their rude red bottoms," complained Frankie.

Actually the baby monkeys really reminded me of my little brother. Not the rude bottoms, I don't mean, but their expressions. They gazed in at us, looking so round-eyed and innocent, they almost made me want to cry. "I think they're super sweet," I said.

"Me too," Kirstin smiled. "Actually my aunt keeps spider monkeys."

"What monkeys?" Lyndz asked, instantly intrigued.

"Spider monkeys are very tiny, the size of a small doll."

"I wonder if Dad would let me have a monkey," mused Lyndz.

"Don't take your eyes off her," I told Kirstin, "or that girl will have a baby monkey zipped inside her hoodie before you know it."

"Is that what happened with the pig?" giggled Kirstin.

"Don't ask," I joked. "I've only just stopped having nightmares."

The monkeys had got bored with trying to steal the windscreen wipers. They crouched on the bonnet of the Landrover and started to style each other's hair. Well, that's what I thought they were doing until our ranger explained they were picking lice out of each other's coats.

"But they're eating them," I protested.

"Lice are very nutritious!" he grinned.

"Too much information," Lyndz said faintly.

Emma gave a prissy giggle. "I must say, I'd really hate to have to eat my own head lice!"

Kenny's eyes gleamed. "Whose would you prefer? Emily's?"

Emma went red. "I'm not going to answer that remark, Laura," she said snootily.

"Ooh, look! That monkey with the big bottom looks exactly like Emily!" Frankie taunted.

"Not that we've ever *seen* Emily's bottom," Kenz sniggered.

I felt a sudden longing to be under the shower, soaping my hair with bubble-gum scented shampoo. Just the thought of lice made my scalp itch like crazy.

Mrs Weaver seemed oddly relieved when the monkeys swung off into the trees at last. "That was fascinating," she said brightly. "But I didn't expect them to come quite so close."

We all exchanged meaningful glances.

Kenny made daring clucking noises under her breath.

Kirstin spluttered with giggles. "You guys are crazy."

After that we drove for ages without seeing anything interesting.

"I want to see a tiger," moaned Frankie.

"I can't see any tigers, but I can spy something black and white that looks amazingly like a horse," Kirstin told her.

"A zebra!" Lyndz shrieked. "My all-time favourite animal."

The zebras looked smaller in real life than they seem on nature programmes. They were more like cute little stripy ponies than horses. The design on their coats was so gorgeous that I couldn't help imagining it on a t-shirt.

"They're so gentle," I said to Kirstin.

"The last time I saw a zebra, it was busy being lunch for a pack of lions," she commented.

Rosie looked horrified. "How awful."

Kenny's eyes gleamed. "It's not awful, it's natural."

"Then I don't think I like Nature," Rosie whispered.

A few minutes later the ranger suddenly killed the engine. "Try to keep your voices down," he whispered, "or we'll scare her off."

A family of tigers was sunbathing under some oak trees.

The mother tiger's orange and black stripes looked incredibly exotic in the spring landscape. She was washing one of her fuzzy little cubs. I saw how her slightest movement rippled the powerful muscles under her coat. The tiger might look peaceful now, but you could feel this electrifying wildness underneath. Everyone was in total awe.

"Is this a dream?" I whispered.

Mrs Weaver shook her head. "If it is, we're having the same one."

"Now I can die happy," breathed Frankie.

"Me too," said Kirstin softly.

Emma looked astonished. "Haven't you seen a tiger before?"

Kirstin shook her head. "Never. You don't get them in Africa. Actually I think tigers are from India."

Emma went slightly pink. I sniggered to myself. Obviously I wasn't the only ten year old who didn't know where tigers came from!

"I've never seen one either," she confessed to Kirstin. "And we come here loads."

The ranger smiled. "Then this must be your lucky day."

You know how cats like to find a patch of sun and chill? Well that's what this very big cat was doing. Her funny little tiger babies were tumbling around her, staging play fights and licking each other's ears.

"They might be killers," Rosie whispered. "But they're the most beautiful creatures on earth."

"I know," I whispered back. "I'm in love."

Our thrilling safari experience came to an end at last and we all clambered out of the Landrover. My bottom was so numb I could hardly stand. Everyone had major pins and needles.

"That was SO perfect!" I said to Rosie happily.

"I can't believe how sweet Emma's being," she said in a low voice. "You can see she's desperate for Kirstin to have a good time."

"Yeah," said Lyndz. "It's like we're seeing a totally new side of her."

Frankie gave her a withering look. "You're such suckers," she said. "Emma's acting, stoopid, just like us. Isn't she, Kenz?"

Kenny wasn't listening. She was still clowning around, pretending her numb legs wouldn't hold her up. Suddenly she tripped and fell over for real. "Ow!!" she yelped. "I landed on a stupid stone."

"Lucky it was your bum," Frankie told her. "It's the fattest part!"

Kenny picked herself up. "Come here and say that!" she threatened.

Suddenly we were all having a mad Keystone Cops moment, as everyone helped

Kenny chase Frankie madly around the grounds, even Emma and Kirstin. Kirstin couldn't run properly because she was laughing so much.

At the last minute, Emma dived on Frankie and brought her to the ground. "Gotcha!" she giggled. "I've ALWAYS wanted to do that!"

I suppose she was still overexcited from seeing the tiger. Or maybe she was a better actress than I'd realised. But just at that moment she looked, well, normal.

Frankie quickly wriggled free. "Have you really, Emma?" she said coldly. "Well, you got that one for free. The next one you'll pay for."

Emma's expression changed. "Is that right?" she said ominously. She scrambled to her feet. Frankie jumped up, dusting off her trousers. Frankie and Emma began to circle each other menacingly, like flamenco dancers.

"I knew you couldn't keep up your sugar and spice act, Emma Hughes," Frankie spat. "Now your true colours are showing."

Kirstin looked puzzled. "What's Frankie talking about?"

Rosie gave a nervous giggle. "Don't ask us.

We're Frankie's friends and we don't understand her half the time, do we, Flissie?"

This is terrible! I thought. They're really going to fight!!

Any minute now they'd be scrapping like wild cats and Operation Pretend Friend would be ruined. I had to do something. Something so bizarre and shocking that Emma and Frankie would temporarily forget about their feud. And then I knew!

"OH! OH! IT'S HORRIBLE!!" I shrieked at the top of my lungs. "OMIGOSH, FRANKIE! YOU WERE RIGHT!"

Frankie froze as she was just about to grab Emma's ponytail.

"What are you on about?" she said nervously.

"I saw it," I invented wildly. "Up there on the turrets! It was horrible!"

"What are you talking about?" Emma gasped.

"The ghost," I lied. "I saw the ghost of Gawdy Castle!"

CHAPTER EIGHT

Ten minutes later the whole class was in the castle grounds, happily tucking into barbecued burgers and bangers.

After a private chat with Mrs Weaver, I'd sheepishly explained that I probably hadn't seen a ghost at all. It was just a trick of the light. The boys were already calling me Casper.

Lyndz was the only person who'd sussed what I was up to.

"That was brilliant, Flissie. Frankie almost blew the whole thing," she whispered. "You do know everyone's going to think you're loopy?"

"It was worth it," I grinned. "Operation You Know What is back on track."

"Ssh," hissed Lyndz. "Kirstin's coming over."

Kirstin's plate was heaped with food. "These are great snags," she mumbled through a mouthful of sausage. "How are you feeling now, Fliss?"

"Better," I said bravely. "You must think I'm a real wally."

"Not at all. I'd have screamed blue murder if I'd seen a ghost."

Frankie finished off her second veggie burger. "She didn't really see one," she sniggered. "She saw a shadow and freaked."

"I got confused," I said defensively. "It could happen to anyone."

"Not me," declared Frankie. "I have nerves of steel!"

"This barbecue is the best," Lyndz said tactfully. "I just lurve eating outdoors, don't you, Emma?"

Emma flicked a beetle away from her sausages. "I suppose. It's not very hygienic."

"It's not very hygienic," Frankie mimicked.

Lyndz hastily talked over her. "What do you think of the food, Kirstin?"

"It's good," she grinned. "Safaris tend to make you hungry."

"What things do you barbecue in Australia? Apart from 'snags'?" Kenny asked her.

Kirstin pulled a face. "Australians will barbecue anything: emu, crocodiles, kangaroo."

"Kangaroo? You're kidding," said Lyndz in horror.

"Have you tried any of those witchetty grubs?" Kenny asked.

"No, I generally stick to the steak," Kirstin laughed.

Mrs Weaver was clapping her hands again.

"We're going around the exotic farm next," Rosie said.

"Whoopdee-do," sighed Kenny. "Like we've never seen a farm."

Kirstin gave Lyndz a sly look. "It says in the book they've got Vietnamese pot-bellied pigs. Lyndz should definitely take a look at those!"

Lyndz shook her head. "Nothing can top that amazing tiger. As far as I'm concerned we can go home."

We knew what she meant. The farm was actually quite cool. The Vietnamese pot-bellied pigs were surprisingly cute and the llamas were hilarious. (They were also VERY whiffy.) But I wished we could have seen them before we had our safari. Our hearts weren't in it somehow.

Lyndz is right, I thought. Nothing's going to come near that tiger.

Kenz was bored. She peered over a low enclosure and a bunch of equally bored-looking peacocks looked back. I vaguely heard Kenz say, "Yo! Peacocks! Can't you do something interesting?"

I wasn't really paying much attention. The fresh air had given me dry lips and I was rubbing on my strawberry lip balm. So I can't actually tell you why that peacock took such a dislike to Kenny. To this day she swears that all she did was say "Yo!"

When I told Andy later, he said, "Was Kenny wearing her Leicester City sweatshirt?" I nodded. "There you go. Mystery solved," he teased. "The peacock must have supported Nottingham Forest!"

Whatever the reason, the peacock launched itself over the wall at Kenny in a fury, rattling its quills like castanets, making hideous screeching noises and trying to peck her in some really personal places. Obviously Kenny didn't want to be pecked to death so she just took off.

Peacocks run a lot faster than you think. This one gave the impression of moving on greased roller skates. And I don't know if you've ever had a good look at a peacock's beak, but it's vicious!

Luckily Kenny's football skills came in handy as she ran around the farmyard, darting this way and that, desperately trying to keep out of the peacock's way.

Honestly it was the maddest thing I've ever seen. We were practically crying with laughter. But the angry peacock showed absolutely no sign of giving up. We started to worry that our mate would get hurt.

"I'd better get someone," I said anxiously.

Kirstin shook her head. "I know what to do!" And she lowered her head like a charging bull and rushed at the peacock, making screamy peacock noises.

You could see the peacock thinking, "Yikes! Too much competition!" It took off for the barn roof, where it settled out of harm's way, glaring down at us with mad, glittery eyes, and making screechy sounds. I got the feeling it was saying "nah nah nah nah nah" in peacock language.

"Thanks, Kirstin," panted Kenny.

"No worries," Kirstin smiled.

Kirstin's cap had fallen off while she was running. Danny McCloud handed it back. "That was well impressive."

"Yeah, we convicts have our uses," she told him.

Unfortunately Mrs Weaver had appeared in the middle of the mayhem. "That bird seems very upset," she said accusingly. "You weren't teasing it, were you?"

"No, Mrs Weaver," we chorused.

But our teacher just said, "Hmmn. We're going to look at the maze now. But I'll be keeping a close eye on you girls for the rest of the day."

"Yes, Mrs Weaver," we sighed.

"She can't keep an eye on us if we're in the maze," Frankie grinned.

I think she was picturing those massive mazes you see in films. The kind where hordes of different characters wander in aimless circles without ever running into each other. But the maze at Gawdy Castle was nothing like that.

"It's diddy!" I gasped.

"The hedges only come up to my knee," said Kenny in disgust.

"Where's the challenge in that?" Frankie agreed.

"I want you to divide into pairs," Mrs Weaver was saying. "The first pair to find their way to the centre in the fastest time wins this bag of Celebration chocolates."

Kenny's eyes gleamed. "That's all the challenge I need!"

We all queued impatiently for our turn to go into the maze. Frankie paired off with Rosie. I went with Kenz and Emma went in with Kirstin.

Lyndz said she'd just watch. She had Lyndz-type plans of her own, but we only found that out later.

It was really tricky going through that maze. You could see the middle all right, but getting there took longer than you'd think. The twists and turns were so tight, you couldn't exactly run fast. Plus I felt like a huge giant jogging along those prickly little paths. The boys got fed up with the whole thing. They treated the hedges like hurdles and hopped over, so Mrs Weaver said they were disqualified.

Emma and Kirstin made the fastest time.

To our amazement Emma offered the chocolates round.

"I couldn't. They're yours!" said Frankie stiffly. I knew how she felt. It did seem unnatural to be taking sweets from our old enemy.

"Take two!" said Kirstin. "They're not ours, dummy, they're the Sleepover Club's."

Frankie still hesitated.

"I didn't poison them, Francesca," Emma snapped.

"Wouldn't put it past you," Frankie muttered.

Lyndz interrupted what could have been a nasty incident. She came hurtling through the grounds, yelling excitedly. "Mrs Weaver, I found where they put that baby elephant and its mum!" she yelled. "Can I take my mates to say hello?"

"Certainly not, Lindsay. We have a packed schedule as you know," Mrs Weaver protested. "There's still the castle to see. Besides after that incident with the peacock—"

To everyone's amazement Emma interrupted. "Please, Mrs Weaver, that wasn't Kenny's fault. The peacock attacked her. All Kenny did was run away. And we'd only be five minutes, wouldn't we?" she asked us.

Teachers treat you quite differently if you're their pet, don't they?

Mrs Weaver instantly changed her tune. "All right, Emma dear. But do be quick. The rest of us will make our way to the castle."

I heard mutterings from the other kids. They wanted to see the elephants too. You could see that Frankie totally didn't want any favours from Emma, but she was also dying to see the baby elephant again, so she had to go along with it.

The mother and baby were in a quiet out-building in near darkness. It felt really peaceful in there. The ranger in the body warmer was chatting to the mother, and feeding her bananas.

She took them in her trunk really carefully and popped them whole into her mouth.

"I see you've brought your mates," he said to Lyndz.

She was already stroking the baby's head, crooning softly. "You'll soon be better, and then you'll be back with all the others."

Lyndz is so nuts about animals it's unbelievable!

The mother finished the last banana and peered around in the gloom, looking for something.

"She's thirsty," her keeper explained.

There was a full bucket of water by the door, so Frankie thoughtfully dragged it over.

"There you go, Mrs Elephant," she said. "Can you reach it now?"

The elephant had a good long guzzle of water, then she studied us all thoughtfully. Afterwards, Frankie swore she'd been smiling.

"You'd better move away!" warned the ranger.

But it was too late. Before we'd realised what she was going to do, the elephant spurted about a gallon of water all over Emma!

It sounds really mean, but we all cracked up. I thought Frankie was going to die actually. She was literally holding her sides and howling with laughter. "Emma, you look just like a drowned rat!"

Poor Emma was soaked through and shivering so I rushed her back to Mrs Weaver.

"Don't worry, dear, I always bring spare clothes on school trips," our teacher comforted her.

But Emma flatly refused to change out of her outfit. She got quite hysterical about it. I think Mrs Weaver thought Emma was worried about strangers seeing her underwear. But I've had time to think about it since then and I don't think it was an underwear problem at all.

I think she thought of her hideous combats as her Sleepover Club clothes. She didn't *like* us really, but she did *admire* us. She was desperate to be one of us, even for a day.

I took Emma back to the coach where I blotted up the worst of the elephant water with paper towels.

"You're a good friend, Fliss," Emma said in a teary voice.

"You're not so bad yourself," I said. "Actually I thought you took that really well. You could have gone ballistic when that elephant drenched you. But you didn't."

"They laughed at me," Emma said miserably.

"Yeah, but it's not personal. We laugh at everyone. We laughed at Kenz. You did too."

Emma cheered up slightly. "I think I'm going to dream about that peacock chasing Kenny! It was the funniest sight I've seen in my life."

"You looked quite funny yourself," I reminded her.

She gave a funny little grin. "I suppose I did. Thanks for helping. I mean it."

"Hurry up, you guys. They're waiting for us outside the castle!" The other Sleepover Club members had come to find us.

Kirstin's eyes were sparkling. "What do you reckon, Fliss? Do you think we'll see anything spooky?"

How is it one little word can totally change your mood? One minute you're sunny and happy and everyone's best friend. Next minute a wormy doubt wriggles into your mind and takes a nasty lump out of your confidence. All because of one word: "SPOOKY".

It had too many "Os". It made me think of ghostly mouths wailing in the dark. "Ooooh! Ooooh! Ooooh!"

A shiver went through me as if someone had just dropped an ice cube down my back. Stop it, Fliss, I told myself firmly. Nothing scary is going to happen in the castle. Frankie's outrageous ghost story wasn't even true, remember?

I tried not to picture a wailing, white-faced ghost pulling a terrified child inside the castle wall.

It couldn't be true. Could it?

CHAPTER NINE

"Not very good-looking, are they," Frankie mused.

"I reckon all the Gawdy family inherited the ugly gene," agreed Kenny.

We were standing in the entrance hall to Gawdy Castle. It was nothing like I'd imagined. It was actually disappointingly ordinary.

The floor was carpeted in a faded rose design that reminded me of my grandma's sitting room. Huge oil paintings of the Gawdy family hung on all the walls.

Nature had been really unkind to them, poor

things. They all had really sticky-out teeth and practically NO chins.

"They're like cartoon characters," I giggled.

"The Gawdys go back for generations," said a disapproving voice. "They're a very fine old English family."

A very pale woman had come up behind us without us noticing. I'm not exaggerating, I don't think I've ever seen such a depressing-looking person. She definitely needs a makeover, I thought. Black is SO not her colour. If she just had a little touch of pink, now it would make all the difference.

Frankie was peering suspiciously behind the woman.

"What are you doing?" I hissed.

"Seeing if she casts a shadow. That woman has to be a vampire."

"I thought they couldn't come out in daylight," I objected.

"This is the part of the tour where your teacher gets a rest." The woman glanced around the class and I thought she was going to smile, but she didn't. "My name is—"

"Dracula?" Frankie muttered.

Luckily the woman didn't seem to hear. "My name is Mrs Skinner and the gentleman standing next to me is Mr Clemency. We're your guides and in a few moments we'll be taking you on a tour of this fascinating old castle."

Mr Clemency was a jolly elderly man with a curly white beard. He twinkled at us over his glasses.

"Oh, that's fair. Not!" hissed Kenny. "Half of us get stuck with Mrs Grim Reaper here, while the rest get Father Christmas!"

"We could get lucky," I said hopefully. "We might get Mr Clemency."

We weren't and we didn't. The lucky fifty per cent of the class walked out into the sunlight with cuddly Mr Clemency. The rest of us followed scary Mrs Skinner up a very gloomy staircase.

"To who knows where," Frankie hissed dramatically.

But in the end our tour guide wasn't sinister so much as boring.

"If I hear one more fact about this castle, I'm going to scream," Kenny complained after half an hour.

"It's her voice," Kirstin explained. "She just drones on. It makes everything sound the same."

It was true. If you actually listened to Mrs Skinner's words she was telling us about genuinely thrilling events, bloody battles and ferocious family feuds. But she could have been reciting stuff out of the telephone book.

Rosie kept looking around nervously. "Are you sensing anything?" she whispered.

"Yeah, I'm sensing my brain is slowly going numb," I whispered back.

"I meant ghosts, stoopid. If anyone's going to see the Gawdy Castle ghost, you would."

"Rosie, I didn't really see a ghost," I explained. "I thought you knew that. I was just trying to stop Emma and Frankie fighting."

"You don't have to pretend, Flissie," said Rosie. "I saw you, remember. You looked terrified."

"I was," I said truthfully. "I was terrified Frankie would bop Emma on the nose and ruin everything." I could see Rosie didn't believe me. "OK, Rosie-posie," I sighed. "If I see the Gawdy Castle ghost, you'll be the first to know."

We continued down yet another corridor lined with portraits of hunting dogs and dead pheasants.

"Doesn't this castle have any dungeons?" Frankie asked our guide.

Everyone perked up. But Mrs Skinner didn't seem to hear. "Now we're going into the kitchens," she droned. "Where there is a bread oven that predates Henry V."

"Wouldn't want to miss that," Frankie said in a sarky voice.

But as we entered the vast barn of a kitchen, Mrs Skinner's walkie-talkie started to hiss and a muffled voice began to speak.

"My feet hurt," Rosie moaned.

"My ears hurt," said Kenny. "From listening to that woman."

Mrs Skinner spoke briefly into her walkie-talkie. "I'm afraid I'll have to cut this tour short to take a personal call in the office," she told us. "Make your way to the reception hall and wait for the others."

And she hurried off without even a backward look.

Everyone gave sighs of relief.

"Excellent," said Frankie. "We can finally have some fun."

Emma looked suspicious. "What kind of fun?"

"Look, there's a map of the castle on the wall there. I bet we've got at least ten minutes until the other group finishes going round." Frankie looked incredibly mischievous. "We can go and explore by ourselves. We can go into the secret rooms they don't want you to know about."

Rosie's eyes grew wide. "You want us to go off on our own?"

"I certainly do," said Frankie. "It's time we had some action."

"But what about the story?" Rosie gasped. "That poor boy who was pulled into the wall?"

"It wasn't true, Rosie," said Emma in her M&Ms voice. "I told you before. It was just a stupid story."

"Bet you'd be scared if it happened to you," said Frankie rudely.

"I wouldn't," said Emma at once. "I can do anything you can, Francesca Thomas."

"Oh, really?" said Frankie. "Then prove it."

The two girls glared at each other.

"Erm, guys," I said.

"Those girls have the weirdest friendship," Kirstin said in my ear. "I mean right now you'd think they hated each other, wouldn't you?"

"Go on, Emma," Frankie was saying. "Prove how brave you are!"

"Keep it down," I whispered. "Everyone's looking."

"Let them," said Frankie. "What use is a dare with no witnesses?"

"A dare!" I gulped. "'What do you mean?"

"I dare Emma to go down into the castle dungeons!" said Frankie loudly.

Everyone gasped.

Emma looked slightly pale, but she said quickly, "Make it a double dare and I'll accept."

"Fine by me," Frankie said in a fierce voice.

To my dismay, Kirstin said, "All the Sleepover Club girls should go. Make it a Sleepover Club Dare," she giggled. "No wimping allowed."

I didn't want any kind of dare. I was totally bewildered. How did this even get started?

Emma was frowning at the wall map. "OK, everyone follow me."

The other kids looked at us in awe. They couldn't believe we were going down to the dungeons on our own, and nor could I.

We followed Emma downstairs and along twisty stone corridors until we were dizzy. Finally we went down a steep flight of steps. At the bottom was a huge, iron-studded door.

"They probably keep it locked," Rosie said hopefully. "If there's a torture chamber down there."

But I knew we weren't that lucky.

It was like that time my little brother tried to put those baby frogs in his pocket. They hopped out and went legging it back to the brook, as fast as he put them in. "I wanted to be their friend," he'd sobbed.

I'd been hoping that if I tried hard enough, everyone would get on. I'd tried so hard I was worn out. And it had been a total waste of time. Now Emma and Frankie were glowering at each other outside a scary medieval dungeon. Any minute now Kirstin would suss what was going on.

Emma turned the knob and triumphantly yanked the door open, straining against its weight. On the other side, worn stone steps disappeared into the dark. Operation Pretend Friend had come to the end of the road.

CHAPTER TEN

"Anyone got a match?" said Emma in a casual voice.

"It's obvious you aren't in the Brownies!" said Frankie contemptuously.

She pushed past Emma, and I saw she was shining a tiny pencil torch. She ducked through the doorway, beaming the narrow ray of light into the dark. Even with the torch it looked horribly creepy. And I could hear sounds of water dripping steadily on stone.

"Well, come on," Frankie called to Emma. "Or everyone will think you're chicken!"

Emma tossed her ponytail and started off down the steps.

I don't think either of them wanted to go into a dungeon which might have been used as a medieval torture chamber. But it had become a matter of honour.

I'm the Sleepover Club wimp as you know, but I couldn't let Frankie do her horrifying dare alone. I took a deep breath and went pattering after her down the steps. I knew Rosie, Kenny and Lyndz were following, because I could hear bizarre snatches of conversation.

"You can share out my new Leicester City kit between you," Kenny whispered. "Take care of it and remember me fondly."

Rosie gave a hysterical giggle. "How can we remember you if we're dead, birdbrain?"

"Don't be stupid," I called to them. "We're going to be fine."

Unfortunately my voice gave a massive wobble in the middle.

"Hurry up, guys!" Frankie yelled. "It's freezing down here!"

"Oh, no! That means it's haunted," Rosie

squeaked. "It's always cold where there are ghosts."

We found ourselves in a kind of crude tunnel that had been carved into the rock. The ceiling was so low there was hardly room to stand. There was only one direction to go. The sign said: This Way To The Dungeons.

As we tiptoed down the dank passage, I thought I heard faint scratching inside the walls. "Do you think they have rats in this castle?" I asked, trying to sound as if I was just inquiring.

"Of course there are, you bozo," said Kenny. "There's always rats in dungeons."

I froze. "Are there?"

"Get a move on, Flissie, or they'll come and nibble your toes," she said impatiently.

"Kenny's joking," said Lyndz in my ear. "It's probably just the heating pipes creaking or something."

We crept cautiously along the passageway, following the weak light of Frankie's torch. Every sound made me break into goose bumps. If we'd been in Mr Clemency's group, we'd have finished our tour by now. We'd be outside in the spring sunshine, sharing out the

Celebration chocolates. Not down here in the damp, smelly dark with invisible rats.

Suddenly someone screamed.

Then I saw the dead body and someone else started screaming and screaming. It took me ages to realise it was me.

The corpse dangled from its chains like a horrible puppet. We all clutched each other gibbering with fear.

Lyndz sounded as if she might be going to be sick. "You can see the blood!" she whispered. "He must have died SO horribly!"

Kirstin squeezed past without a word and went to inspect the body. It's unbelievable how cool Australians are in a crisis. "Hmmn," she said. "I thought it was well-preserved for a corpse. A medieval torture victim should be dust and bones by now."

We stared at her in the flickering torchlight.

"Relax, you guys!" she chuckled. "It's a waxwork. They probably used to run scary dungeon tours or something. Not very good ones by the look of this guy."

I felt such an idiot. Now I really came to look, the dead body was obviously a dummy.

I could tell Emma felt really embarrassed too.

"I knew it wasn't real," she said quickly.

"Is that why you held on so tightly you practically broke my arm?" Frankie sneered.

"I did not," Emma snapped.

Kirstin was groping her way along the tunnel. "There's a door at the end," she called. "What do you reckon we'll find in here?"

"Don't bother," said Kenny gloomily. "It'll just be another stupid dummy."

"Hey, I've come all the way from Australia for this," Kirstin said cheerfully. "I want my money's worth."

She lifted the old-fashioned latch on the door, then suddenly staggered back.

"Are you OK?" asked Frankie.

Kirstin shook her head. "I'm not sure. The door felt so cold," she whispered. "It was so cold it hurt."

"I think we should go now," Lyndz said in a rather high voice. "I think we should go back to the others."

Emma gave Frankie a wary look. "If I go it's not because I'm scared," she gulped.

Frankie shook her head. "Me neither."

But before anyone could move. Kirstin began to shiver violently. "It's so cold," she moaned. "And everything's going so dark."

To our horror, she crumpled to the floor, still moaning faintly.

"What's wrong with her?" Emma squeaked.

"I think she had some kind of fainting fit." Frankie sounded genuinely scared. "You're the medical person, Kenny. What should we do?"

"I'm going to get Mrs Weaver," Kenny whispered. "Kirstin could be seriously ill."

"NO."

Considering she'd just fainted, Kirstin's voice sounded really loud and strange. She rose very slowly to her feet. "Stay where you are, mortal!" she boomed.

Something had definitely happened to Kirstin's voice. It sounded deeper and harsher. Her face looked different too. Kind of stern and unfriendly.

"You should probably sit down," said Emma nervously. "Maybe you don't remember, but you fainted."

"I am perfectly well, now I have this mortal's body," Kirstin said in her new scary voice.

I had a very creepy feeling. Something really weird had happened to Kirstin. Something supernatural-weird.

"What do you mean you've got her body?" Frankie quavered.

"Quiet!" said the voice. "Or I will crush your pathetic bones to pulp!"

Lyndz whimpered and covered her eyes.

"Who – who are you?" stammered Emma.

"I am an unquiet spirit. My life was taken in this dungeon and now I want your blood in revenge!"

That's all we needed to hear. We picked up our heels and ran screaming from the dungeon. I fell over and landed on my knees hard. But I didn't care about the pain or that I might be bleeding on my new jeans. I just wanted to get out of the dark and back to safety. We ran up the stairs, into the reception hall and straight into Mrs Skinner.

"Girls, girls, what's all this?"

Everyone was babbling hysterically. Frankie was actually crying.

"It's my fault!" she wept. "If I hadn't dared Emma, the unquiet spirit wouldn't have got Kirstin!"

Mrs Skinner looked baffled. "Who got who? What are you talking about?"

"The ghost of Gawdy Castle," Frankie wailed.

Mrs Skinner looked surprised. "But Maude wouldn't hurt a fly."

Frankie's tears stopped like magic. Everyone stared at Mrs Skinner.

"You mean the castle is really haunted?" I asked.

"Of course. Most old places are. But the Gawdy Castle ghost is quite harmless."

"But we SAW it in the dungeons!" Emma wailed.

The tour guide clicked her tongue. "I'm not going to ask what you were doing there. But you certainly won't find Maude in the dungeons. I usually see her in the hall or the rose garden."

"The ghost is called Maude?" Kenny seemed disgusted.

"What about Kirstin," Emma pleaded. "I'm really worried about her. Something awful happened down there."

"It's like she was possessed by a demon!" Frankie agreed.

"Yeah, I really had you going, eh?" laughed a voice.

Kirstin was sauntering towards us, giving absolutely no sign of being possessed by a demon.

Frankie's mouth fell open. "NO way! You DIDN'T!!"

"I did!" grinned Kirstin. "I played you for suckers and you swallowed it hook, line and sinker!"

I looked down at my knees. For the first time I noticed the blood seeping through the denim. I was officially angry with Kirstin. "I'm glad you think it's so funny. Now I've got to tell Mum I've ruined my new jeans."

"I'm sorry about your jeans, Fliss," she said. "But I truly didn't think you'd run out so quickly. I was just going to own up when you all took off like a bunch of lemmings!"

One thing about Frankie is she's an excellent sport. She gave an embarrassed laugh. "That was a pretty cool trick," she admitted grudgingly. "For an Australian."

"I'd love to have seen us on video," agreed Kenny. "I bet we were white as sheets!"

"You were!" giggled Kirstin.

"And that voice was well spooky!" said Frankie.

The word reminded me that Gawdy Castle actually had a real ghost.

"Mrs Skinner, have you seen Maude?" I asked nervously.

"Oh, you never see her. You know she's there though. You can smell lavender in the air and you sometimes hear long skirts rustling."

Rosie sighed. "That sounds like my kind of ghost."

"I hope your phone call wasn't bad news, Mrs Skinner," I said shyly.

Mrs Skinner looked surprised. "How sweet of you to ask. Actually it was very good news. My daughter has just had a baby. We've been worried about them both. But they're perfectly fine!"

We all congratulated her and told her she didn't look nearly old enough to be a granny, though like Kenny said later, it's not that easy to tell with the undead!

We were just getting back on the coach when I realised I'd left my sweatshirt in the reception hall.

"Keep my seat for me," I told the others. "I'll be back in two ticks," and I went haring back to the castle.

At first I couldn't see my top anywhere, then I found it crumpled behind a radiator in the hall. It was really grimy from the dungeons. Mum's going to think I've been in a war, I thought. I've ruined my new jeans and my sweatshirt looks like a dusty old relic from a museum.

Just then I heard the soft swish of a woman's skirt behind me.

"Oh, Mrs Skinner," I said guiltily. "I was just—"

But when I turned the hall was empty, and I could smell the sweet scent of lavender.

CHAPTER ELEVEN

That night we prepared for the most bizarre sleepover ever.

You see, on the way back on the coach, it came out that Kirstin was going to be leaving Cuddington next week. Her parents were dragging her off to some big ecological project down in Cornwall.

"I'm gutted," she said. "If I'd been here a few days longer Emma could have brought me to one of your famous sleepovers!"

Frankie took a huge breath and my heart literally stopped as I waited for her to drop Emma right in the poo! I don't really know why she didn't. Maybe it was because she could see Kirstin was genuinely disappointed.

Frankie leaned across to Emma and tapped lightly on her skull. "Hello! Anyone at home?" She laughed. "Poor Emma. She's losing it, aren't you, Emma? I can't believe she forgot to tell you."

"Forgot to tell her what?" said Emma nervously, obviously suspecting some new insult.

"Duh! We're sleeping over at Fliss's tonight, dummy! We'll see you guys there, won't we, Fliss?"

My head was spinning with surprise. "Oh, yeah," I croaked. "Erm, don't forget to bring sleeping bags."

"And a spooky story and food for your midnight feast, right?" grinned Kirstin. "Emma's told me all about it."

"I don't believe you did that, Frankie Thomas," Kenny burst out, as Emma and Kirstin went off in Emma's mum's car.

"YOU can't believe I did it! I'm not going to sleep a wink, knowing I'm under the same roof as that girl." Frankie looked genuinely panicky. "I'm really, really sorry guys. I just didn't know what else to do."

"No, you did right, Spaceman," Kenny comforted her. "It's not Kirstin's fault Emma's been telling all these lies."

"Anyway, how bad can it be?" said Rosie bravely.

"Just don't go leaking any crucial Sleepover Club secrets," Kenny warned.

But our fears proved totally groundless. When Emma's mum's car stopped outside our house later that evening, just one girl got out.

I ran to the door to let Kirstin in. "Where's Emma?"

"It's such a shame! She couldn't come. She's really not feeling well."

"Don't say she's caught Emily's nits after all?"

Kirstin shook her head. "She's just got a chill. She did get a bit of a soaking."

Maybe Emma's illness was genuine. But I also think she was scared. She must have known she couldn't keep up the pretence of being a bona fide member of the Sleepover Club. Not once she was on our territory.

Emma really did us a big favour. We agreed later that our safari sleepover would have been seriously stressful if she'd been there, with her prissy voice and her pulled-back ponytail.

But we didn't say any of this to Kirstin. We were too busy stuffing ourselves with the Cheesy Doritos she'd brought, and reminiscing about our mad experiences at Gawdy Castle.

Kirstin told us she'd half-sussed that Emma wasn't exactly our big bosom buddy, like she'd claimed in her e-mails. But she was truly astonished when we explained that Emily Berryman was Emma's real friend. "She never even mentioned her! I wonder why?"

"You'd have to know Emily to understand that," said Kenny darkly.

Kirstin has to be one of the coolest girls I've ever met. She had no illusions about Emma, but she totally refused to diss her. "Emma has some good points," she said. "And she's obviously nuts about you guys."

I thought about that a lot as I finally snuggled down in my sleeping bag. We didn't do the tent thing in the end, by the way. Even Frankie agreed that we'd had more than enough excitement for one day.

I could hear Andy upstairs talking soothingly to one of the twins, or he could have been reciting his list of builders' tools. But it still sounded comforting and homey.

As I drifted off to sleep, I wondered why Emma really told Kirstin those stories about her imaginary sleepover experiences. We'd never know. Next term Emily would be back at school and everything would be back to normal. But I couldn't help wondering. Had it all just been acting like Frankie said, or did Emma Hughes really want to be our friend?

Order Form

To order direct from the publishers, just make a list of the titles you want and fill in the form below:

Name ....

Address ....

....

....

Send to: Dept 6, HarperCollins Publishers Ltd, Westerhill Road, Bishopbriggs, Glasgow G64 2QT.

Please enclose a cheque or postal order to the value of the cover price, plus:

UK & BFPO: Add £1.00 for the first book, and 25p per copy for each additional book ordered.

Overseas and Eire: Add £2.95 service charge. Books will be sent by surface mail but quotes for airmail despatch will be given on request.

A 24-hour telephone ordering service is available to holders of Visa, MasterCard, Amex or Switch cards on 0141- 772 2281.

HarperCollins *Children's Books*